# CALCULATOR ANNIE

Annie, who has always been hopeless at even the simplest sums, wakes up one morning to discover she has turned into a mathematical genius. To everyone's amazement, she can now do the most difficult calculations in the world—and in a few seconds too! Annie finds herself helping out at the bank and at the local newspaper, and even gets entered for a competition. But will her extraordinary talent last?

# CALCULATOR ANNIE

Alexander McCall Smith

*Illustrated by*
Jon Riley

*Galaxy*

## CHIVERS PRESS
## BATH

First published 1992
by
Young Corgi Books
This Large Print edition published by
Chivers Press
by arrangement with
1996

ISBN 0 7451 4732 1

British Library Cataloguing in Publication Data

McCall Smith, Alexander, 1948–
  Calculator Annie.—Large print ed.—
  (Galaxy Children's Large Print)
  1. Children's stories, English
  I. Title  II. Series  III. Riley, Jon
  823.9′14 [J]

  ISBN 0–7451–4732–1

*This book is for*
*Rachel and Caroline Wood*

# CALCULATOR ANNIE

# CHAPTER ONE

Annie was by no means stupid. She could tell you the capital cities of at least twenty countries. She could tell you the name of the highest mountain in Nepal, and she could give you the date of George Washington's birthday. In fact, she knew quite a lot.

But when it came to mathematics, Annie was not very good. In fact, she was hopeless. Most people know that 6 multiplied by 2 is 12—but not Annie. And most people can do simple additions like 3 plus 5 plus 2 (which, as you know, makes 10)—but not Annie. In fact, if you asked Annie any question which had anything to do with mathematics she would turn pale and begin to stutter.

'Now, Annie,' said her teacher. 'Can you tell me what 4 plus 8 makes?'

Annie turned red.

'10?' she said after a while. Then, when everyone began to groan, she quickly suggested: '14? No, 16. That's it—16!'

1

'Oh, Annie!' exclaimed her teacher in exasperation. 'Surely you can do a simple sum like that by now!'

But Annie could not. And no matter how hard she tried (and she tried very hard to learn mathematics) she still found it impossible.

They gave her extra lessons. They gave her special books, and when neither of these worked they asked for a visit from an expert who knew a great deal about people who could not do mathematics.

She gave Annie some tests, and in all of them she scored 0 out of 120. This was the worst score the expert had ever seen and she went away shaking her head in dismay.

'That girl is quite hopeless,' she said. 'I'm sorry to have to say this, but it's the truth. She'll never be able to do mathematics. Never!'

Although everybody was sad to hear this said, they knew that it was true. Some people will never be able to dance. Some people will never be able to sing. Some people will just never be able to add, subtract or multiply. Annie was clearly one of those. Not being able to do

2

mathematics has its problems. When Annie went into a shop to buy something, she had to hope that she gave the right money. Sometimes she gave far too little, and the shopkeeper would look at her in a curious way. Sometimes she gave far too much, and the shopkeeper would wonder what was wrong with a girl of her age who couldn't even do a simple thing like hand over the right sum of money. Poor Annie! She felt so foolish when this happened, and yet she knew it really was not her fault. After all, she did try her best.

The worst part of all was the homework. Annie managed to finish most of her homework quite quickly, but the mathematics part of it seemed to take hours. And at the end of all those hours of effort, everything would be wrong—everything!

One evening, Annie was sitting at the kitchen table trying to work out what her mathematics homework was all about. She was getting nowhere when she noticed that her father had left his little electronic calculator on the table. Now you would have thought that a calculator would be the answer to Annie's problems, but this was not so. She had tried in the past to work things out on a calculator, but she had never succeeded. Annie was so hopeless at mathematics that she even went wrong with a calculator. It made no difference at all. When she put $5 + 5$ into the calculator, the answer 15 came up on the screen. And when she keyed in $20 \times 2$ (which is 40 of course), the calculator said 62!

Annie reached over and picked up the

calculator.

'Now,' she said to herself. 'If three men take two weeks to dig a ditch one hundred yards long, then how many men will it take to dig a ditch two hundred yards if the ditch is to be completed in one week?'

What a question! Poor Annie had no idea where to start. She also had no idea why anybody could possibly want to know the answer to a question like that. Surely it depended on the men. Some men dig quickly, others sit on their shovels and look at their boots. And it would also depend on the ground. Mud is quicker than hard clay. And what if they struck rock? These were just the sort of things which mathematics teachers appeared to ignore completely.

Annie tapped a few numbers into the calculator. 2 men × 3 divided by 100? Would that give the answer? She thought she could at least try, and she did. But a very strange answer came out. 16789, said the calculator.

'It's no use,' muttered Annie. 'It's no help at all.'

With a sigh, Annie rose to her feet and

went upstairs to bed. She entered her room and turned on the light. For some reason she found that she still had the calculator in her hand, but she was far too tired to take it downstairs. So she slipped it under her pillow, to remind herself to give it back to her father the next morning.

Annie did not know it, of course, but she had forgotten to turn off the calculator, and all that night the little machine stayed on, glowing away under the pillow. And something very strange happened, although it was not until the next day that Annie was to find out just how strange it was.

# CHAPTER TWO

When the teacher saw Annie's efforts at her mathematics homework she let out a sigh. She tried to understand what Annie had written, but it was all quite wrong, right from the beginning. So the teacher, as usual, just wrote: 'Wrong, wrong, wrong! 0 out of 10, again!' and closed Annie's book.

That was not unusual, but what happened next was very strange. The whole class now moved on to mental arithmetic. The teacher asked a complicated sum and the person who could give the answer first was awarded a point. It was a sort of mathematical game, really, and those members of the class who were good at mathematics really enjoyed it. This was their chance to show off. For Annie, though, it was just another chance to be ashamed of her hopelessness with numbers.

'Right,' said the teacher. 'Without writing anything down, please do the following sum: 20 plus 12 plus 8, minus

5, minus 3, plus 71, minus 16. Answer?'

Everybody closed their eyes and frowned. It was difficult to remember all the numbers and to juggle them about in your head. Annie usually couldn't remember even the first of the figures, let alone add them up.

A hand shot up.

'Somebody has the answer,' said the teacher. Then, looking up, she saw that the somebody was Annie.

'Annie!' she exclaimed. 'Is there something wrong? Do you need to leave the room?'

'87,' said Annie.

'I beg your pardon,' said the teacher. 'Did you say something?'

'87,' repeated Annie. 'I said 87. That's the answer.'

The teacher laughed. 'How strange,' she said. 'You've guessed the answer correctly, Annie. What a funny thing. I suppose you just spoke the first number you thought of.'

Annie said nothing. The teacher, though, asked another question.

'Tell me what the answer is to this: 34 multiplied by 62,' she asked.

A hand shot up. It was Annie's. This time the teacher seemed a little bit annoyed.

'Now, Annie,' she said. 'You mustn't disturb the class like that.'

'2,108,' said Annie.

The teacher turned pale.

'Would you repeat that?' she asked, looking at a small slip of paper she had in her hand.

'2,108,' said Annie, ignoring the

9

whispering of the others in the class. 'That's the answer isn't it?'

'Er ... yes,' said the teacher. '2,108. Yes. That's the answer.'

Everyone now stared at Annie.

'She's cheating, miss,' said an unpleasant boy who sat near Annie. 'She must have pinched the questions before you asked them.'

Annie was outraged.

'I'm not cheating,' she protested. 'I got the answers out of my head.'

The teacher looked at her suspiciously.

'But, my dear,' she said calmly, 'you've never even been able to add 4 and 6. How could you possibly do these sums?'

Annie shrugged her shoulders. 'I've become better at mathematics,' she said. 'I don't know why. I just seem to know the answers.'

She turned to the unpleasant boy.

'And I'm not cheating,' she said. 'I'm really not!'

The teacher told them to stop arguing.

'Let's see,' she said. 'Here's another one. If it takes a crocodile ten minutes to eat a boy weighing one hundred pounds, how long will it take two crocodiles to eat three boys weighing eighty pounds each?'

Annie looked up at the ceiling. The answer came into her mind—just like that. She didn't really have to think.

'Twelve minutes,' she called out. And then added: 'Poor boys!'

The teacher scribbled a few calculations on the board.

'Well!' she said. 'I'm most surprised. Twelve minutes is the answer.'

She paused. 'But here's one I'm sure you won't be able to answer, Annie. Are you ready?'

Annie nodded.

'Right,' began the teacher. 'Divide 2,476,322 by 582, and then, when you've

done that, multiply your answer by 8.'

Everybody gasped as Annie gave her answer.

'34038.789,' she said.

The teacher looked astounded. 'This is quite extraordinary,' she muttered. 'I really don't know what to do.'

# CHAPTER THREE

'Now, everybody!' said the teacher, trying to quieten the buzz of excited chatter which had broken out. 'I want you all to carry on with your work while I'm out of the room. I shall be back in a minute.'

The moment the teacher left the room, everybody turned round to stare at Annie.

'I'll tell you what we should do,' one of Annie's classmates said. 'If you've suddenly become so good at mathematics Annie, then we'll test you.'

'Good idea!' shouted somebody else. 'Let's work out a really difficult sum on paper and then ask Annie to give us the answer.'

Everybody thought this was a good idea. Figures were noted down on paper and the calculation was done. Then, when the answer had been checked and double-checked, one of the boys read out the problem.

'What,' he said, 'is 2,456 multiplied by

67, when the answer is divided by 34?'

'She'll never get that,' somebody whispered. 'It's impossible to work that out in your head—especially if you're Annie!'

Everybody laughed, and while they were laughing they didn't hear Annie's voice.

'4,839,' she said quietly. 'Or, to be exact, 4,839.7647.'

'Her lips moved,' said somebody. 'Come on! What did you say Annie?'

Annie repeated the answer. The boy holding the piece of paper checked what had been written on it. Then his jaw dropped open.

'I don't believe it!' he exclaimed. 'She's right!'

It was only a moment or two after this that the teacher returned. She was not alone—with her was the head teacher, a tall person with glasses that perched on the end of her nose.

'Now,' said the head teacher. 'Which of you is Annie?'

Annie stood up. She felt a bit embarrassed by all this attention. Nobody had ever noticed her much when she was no good at mathematics, and she could not understand what all the fuss should be about now that she seemed to have improved a little.

The head teacher walked up to Annie's desk and peered at her through her glasses.

'I hear that you've made great progress in mathematics,' she said. 'Is that so?'

Annie nodded, feeling rather miserable.

'Then perhaps you would show me,' the head teacher said. 'May I ask you a question?'

'Yes,' said Annie, her voice sounding timid and weak. Everybody was silent now, listening to every word that was said.

'Well,' began the head teacher. 'Let me see.'

She stroked her chin for a moment before continuing.

'Let us say that I have 546 plums in a sack. I give 312 to my friend Harry and then I divide the rest between my friends Jill and Rachel. How many do Jill and Rachel each receive?'

Hardly a second before the head teacher had finished speaking Annie came up with the answer.

'117 each,' she said. And then she added: 'That is, if Jill and Rachel each get the same number.'

The head teacher said nothing for a moment as she tried to work out the answer. About a minute later she came up with it in her head. It was, of course, 117, which was exactly what Annie had said.

The head teacher gasped.

'Quite remarkable,' she said. 'And it is particularly extraordinary in one who used to get 0 in every mathematics examination. However, here's another question.'

She paused, concentrating on the sum she was making up in her head. At last she asked:

'What is 678 multiplied by 4,567?'

Annie stared straight ahead of her as she gave the answer. Once again, the answer was given within a second or two of the question having been asked and, when the head teacher had worked it all out on a piece of paper, Annie's answer proved to be exactly right.

The head teacher drew Annie's teacher aside and the two of them had a whispered conversation. Then the head teacher left, smiling at Annie as she did so. Nobody had heard what the two teachers had said, except for the unpleasant boy.

'You know what the head teacher called you,' he whispered to Annie. 'She called you a "mathematical genius".'

'So what?' said Annie coolly.

'Well,' said the unpleasant boy. 'I wouldn't like to be called a genius. It sounds terrible.'

Annie looked at him scornfully.

'Don't worry,' she said. 'Nobody will ever call you a genius.'

Annie, of course, knew what the word genius meant. She knew that a genius was a person who could do something far, far better than anybody else. Well, if she was a mathematical genius, then that was a nice change. For one thing, mathematics homework need never be a problem again, and that, she had to admit, was a very comforting thought indeed.

# CHAPTER FOUR

From that day onwards, Annie's life was changed. The head teacher arranged for her to be moved into the most senior mathematics class in the school. The people there were very much older than Annie—in fact, they were just about to leave school altogether—but even in spite of this Annie was very much better at the subject than they were. She did all the mathematics exercises in no time at all, and on every occasion she was correct.

Her parents were astonished by the change.

'Whatever happened to you?' her mother asked. 'You used to be so weak at mathematics but now...'

Annie shrugged. 'I just became good at maths,' she answered. She knew of course that it was something to do with sleeping with the calculator under her pillow, but she thought if she said anything about that there might be a terrible fuss. People would probably say

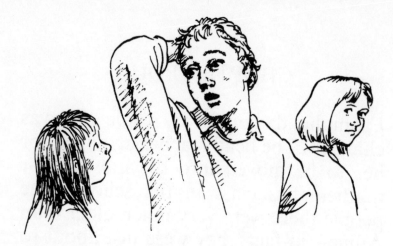

that she was a cheat, or something like that. So she said nothing about the strange way in which she had suddenly become so good at numbers.

Her father did say something about the calculator, though.

'Has anybody seen my little calculator?' he asked one evening. 'It seems to have gone missing.'

'It was on the kitchen table,' Annie's mother said. 'That's where I last saw it.'

'Annie,' said her father. 'You do your homework there sometimes. Do you know where my calculator is?'

Annie gulped. 'I've borrowed it,' she said. 'Could I keep it for a little while longer? It's really helping me with my mathematics.'

Annie's father shook his head. 'I'm afraid I use it all the time,' he said. 'If you need one, we can get you one of your own. They're not expensive, you know.'

Annie did not know what to say. There was something very special about her father's calculator—and she couldn't be sure that any other calculator would have the same effect. In fact, she was sure that it wouldn't.

Just as she was about to ask him whether he wouldn't let her have the old one while he bought a new one, the telephone rang and her father went off to answer it.

'That call was about you,' he said to Annie. 'It was the head teacher at your school. She's putting you in for a mathematics exam—the most difficult one there is. And she's quite sure you'll pass with flying colours.'

He looked at Annie in a rather curious way.

'You haven't always been good at mathematics,' he said, sounding rather puzzled. 'In fact, I thought it was your weakest subject.'

21

'It used to be,' said Annie. 'But I seem to have got a little bit better recently.'

The telephone call had made her father forget about the calculator, and nothing more was said about it. Annie heaved a sigh of relief but she still felt anxious. Everything depended on that calculator, and if she ever lost it, then presumably she would go back to being bad at mathematics. And that, she thought, is something she didn't want to do.

So every night, before she went to bed, she carefully gave the calculator a little polish with a handkerchief and turned it on. Then she slipped it under her pillow, where it lay all night, doing its magic, making her more and more brilliant at mathematics.

*     *     *

The time for the examination arrived. Annie went into the examination hall and sat at a desk. Everybody else stared at her as she came in, which is not surprising—they were all at least eighteen and she was only eleven.

She looked at the examination paper. There was nothing difficult about it—at least, from Annie's point of view—and she started to write the answers straight away. Within ten minutes she had finished.

'Yes?' asked the teacher when Annie went up to her desk at the head of the hall. 'What is it?'

'I've finished,' Annie said, handing her her paper.

The teacher gasped.

'But that's impossible,' she said. 'This is a three hour examination.'

'But I really have finished,' said Annie. 'Look.'

The teacher looked at Annie's paper. All the answers were laid out clearly and correctly. She had undoubtedly completed the whole test.

As Annie left the hall, the eyes of all the others were fixed on her.

'Who does she think she is?' one girl said to another. 'She's just showing off!'

'No,' whispered her neighbour. 'That's Annie—you know, the girl they say is a mathematical genius.'

'I see,' sighed her friend. 'Well, if only I were a genius.'

And with that they turned their heads back to the examination. The questions were really very difficult and they were all finding the going very tough indeed.

\*    \*    \*

It was two weeks before the results of the examination were received. Then, on the day when the results were due to be given to the candidates, the head teacher received a letter from the organizers of the examination.

'I'm afraid your pupils did not do very well,' the letter said, 'except for one. This girl did better than anybody has ever done before in this examination. In fact, not only did she get everything correct, she found a mistake in the examination paper. We are quite astounded.'

The letter went on to give the details of the results and then, at the end, there was something more about Annie.

'We are so impressed,' the letter went on, 'that we have told the newspaper. The editor sounded very interested and has promised that a reporter will call on Annie to interview her. And there will also be a photographer to take her picture. So please ask her to be ready next Friday at half past three.'

# CHAPTER FIVE

The reporter arrived at exactly half past three. With him was the newspaper photographer, with all his complicated camera equipment draped round his neck. As the reporter sat down and began to talk to Annie, the photographer prowled round the room, looking for the best angle for his pictures.

Annie was worried that the reporter would ask her how she became so good at mathematics, or that he might even accuse her of cheating, just as the boys at school had done. But he suggested no such thing, and spent all his time asking her about what she wanted to do in the future.

At the end of the interview he threw in a question—a mathematical one—and Annie answered it immediately and with no effort. The reporter whistled.

'My goodness!' he exclaimed. 'That *was* quick!' He paused, looking sideways at Annie.

'I've just realized that you could help us a great deal,' he said shyly. 'That is, if you wanted to.'

Annie smiled. 'Of course I'll help you,' she said. 'But how?'

The reporter bent down and whispered in Annie's ear.

'We run a competition,' he said. 'It's called The Brainteaser. The readers have to answer a very difficult question, which sometimes involves a lot of mathematical calculation.'

'Well?' said Annie expectantly.

The reporter looked even more embarrassed.

'We've lost the answer,' he whispered. 'The man who set this week's problem has forgotten how to solve the problem he himself set, and we've now lost the piece of paper on which he had written the answer in the first place!'

Annie could not help laughing.

'So you don't know who's won?' she asked.

'Precisely,' said the reporter. 'And it's very embarrassing, believe me!'

Annie thought for a moment.

'I think I know what you want me to do,' she said. 'You want me to . . .'

'Absolutely,' whispered the reporter. 'In fact, could you possibly come down to the newspaper offices right now and sort the whole mess out?'

\*　　\*　　\*

At the newspaper office Annie was introduced to the editor, who shook her hand warmly.

'It's so good of you to help,' he said. 'I was just about to invent an answer.'

28

They showed Annie the problem, as it had been printed in last week's newspaper. Annie studied it, and scratched her head.

'This certainly isn't easy,' she said. 'In fact, it's quite ... brainteasing.'

The editor and the reporter exchanged nervous glances, but they both looked relieved when Annie suddenly reached for a piece of paper and scribbled down a figure.

'That's it,' she said firmly. 'This is your answer.'

While the editor looked at the answer which Annie had come up with, the reporter went off to fetch the box of entry forms sent in by the readers. Then, spreading them out on the table, the three of them went through each form to see who had given the correct answer.

The task of examining all the entries took quite some time, but eventually every one of them had been scrutinized.

'Well,' said the editor, rubbing his eyes. 'I found nobody with the right answer.'

'And neither did I,' said the reporter. 'In fact, everybody was way, way out.'

The two men turned and looked at Annie.

'Well?' said the editor. 'You must have found the winner.'

But Annie shook her head. Not a single entry form had been correct.

The editor looked at the reporter and the reporter looked at the editor. For a moment or two, nobody said anything, but then the editor cleared his throat.

'You may think this is a problem,' he said. 'You may think we don't have a winner. But...' he paused, raising a finger in the air. 'But we do have a winner! There is one person who got the

answer right, and that, Annie, is you!'

Annie was rather surprised, but she understood what the editor meant. Although she had not intended to win, or even to enter the competition, she supposed that she had got it right after all. And if she was the only person to do that, then why shouldn't she be the winner?

'Congratulations!' said the reporter, reaching forward to shake Annie's hand. 'Well done!'

'I do hope you like the prize,' said the editor, handing Annie a cheque. 'I know it's not an awful lot of money, but you should be able to buy yourself something with it. And thank you so much for helping us—we shall be very careful with the answers in future!'

Annie had tea and cakes with the editor and the reporter before leaving. Then, her prize tucked safely away in her pocket, she made her way down the street to the bank.

# CHAPTER SIX

There was a long line of people in the bank, all waiting for service from the tellers. Annie took her place in the queue and watched as the people at the counters transacted their business.

For some reason or other, everything seemed painfully slow. The tellers were working as quickly as they could, but it was not quickly enough. Most of the customers were being patient, but it was clear to Annie that many of them were fed up.

'I've been standing here for almost half an hour,' one woman said angrily. 'And I'm still standing here!'

'You're quite right,' said the man behind her. 'I've got to get some money to go to a sale, but by the time I get there there'll be nothing left.'

'It's quite disgraceful,' agreed another. 'This must be the slowest bank in the world!'

The manager of the bank, who was standing behind the counter watching the tellers, was most upset to hear the customers complaining. Eventually after somebody had threatened to walk out if he was not served in two minutes, the manager came out to explain to the customers.

'I'm terribly sorry,' he said. 'Our computer has broken down. We rely on it so much these days that we're quite lost if it goes wrong.'

'That's the trouble with computers,' one of the customers grumbled. 'If you only used people then you wouldn't have this problem.'

The manager spun round.

'That's where you're wrong, sir,' he said sharply. 'No person is as quick as a computer. Nobody in the world.'

Annie looked around her. Should she say something? Dare she say something? Why not?

'I am,' she said.

When they heard Annie say this, everybody laughed.

'What a funny thing to say,' exclaimed the manager. 'Are you a little bit ... little bit ... odd in the head?'

'I'm quite serious,' said Annie firmly.

'And if you let me show you, you'll see what I can do.'

'Oh what nonsense!' chortled the manager. 'But thank you for cheering us up with your funny little remark!'

'It's not meant to be funny,' said Annie. 'Let me show you. I might even be able to get everybody served.'

'Come on,' said one of the customers. 'Give her a try. Maybe she's one of these mathematical geniuses or something like that.'

The manager seemed uncertain, but when one or two of the other customers urged him on, he realized that here was a convenient way of keeping everybody's mind off the delay.

'Very well,' he said to Annie. 'If you would care to come this way?'

With all the customers peering to see what was going on, Annie was led by the manager to a large metal cabinet behind the counter.

'This is the computer,' he said, giving it a little kick with his shoe to show how he felt about it. 'A person sits here and feeds in the figures from all these cheques and papers which the tellers have. Then

the computer gives out a code and lets
the teller know if there's enough money
in the account. Without the computer, it
all has to be done in the tellers' heads,
and that takes ages.'

Annie looked around her and drew up
a chair.

'Right,' she said in a loud voice. 'The
tellers can pass over each cheque as it's
handed over the counter. I'll look
through all these figures here and tell the
tellers what to do.'

The manager shook his head.

'Impossible,' he said. 'The sums

35

involved are far too big. Nobody could
do that.'

'Let her try,' shouted a customer.
'Anything is worth trying in this rotten
old bank!'

The manager seemed shocked by this
comment, and he signalled to the tellers
to do as Annie had suggested. Annie sat
back, and the task began.

It worked. With lightning speed Annie
gave the tellers the answers they needed.
They, in turn, were able to deal with the
customers quickly, and within minutes
everybody had been served and had

what they wanted. But they didn't leave the bank; as each customer collected his or her money, the crowd of fascinated onlookers swelled. Finally, when the last customer was served, Annie did the final sum in her head, cashed her own prize cheque from the bank, and started to leave.

'Don't go!' pleaded the bank manager. 'You're a genius! You can't just disappear!'

'No,' shouted a voice in the crowd. 'You must be tested. We must see if you're really a mathematical genius.'

'Who can do that?' asked the manager. 'Does anybody know?'

'Yes,' called out a woman from the back. 'My neighbour is the person to see. He's called Professor Prime, and he's a mathematical genius himself. We can all go there right now and ask him to sort this out.'

# CHAPTER SEVEN

Off they all went—the manager, the crowd, Annie and the lady who knew Professor Prime. The lady rang the bell, and when the Professor answered she introduced Annie.

'This girl is called Annie,' she said. 'We found her in the bank, and she's terribly, terribly good at mathematics. Not as good as you, Professor, of course, but still really rather good.'

'So!' the Professor said, looking short-sightedly at Annie. 'So, you're Annie.'

'Yes,' said Annie timidly. 'I am.'

'Well then,' said Professor Prime. 'Can you tell me what is 34,567 multiplied by 82 and one half?'

No more than half a second had passed before Annie replied.

'2,851,777.5,' she said.

Professor Prime looked astonished. Then, when he had recovered his composure, he let out a whoop of delight.

'And what is 76,895 divided by 42?' he cried. 'Tell me that, if you please.'

Annie smiled as she rattled off the answer.

'1830.33333333333333,' she said. And then added: 'The threes go on for ever.'

Professor Prime gave a little hop of pleasure.

'The recurring three!' he exclaimed. 'Yes! You can never get rid of them. They go on and on and on.'

He beamed at Annie. 'If you find you can't get to sleep,' he said, 'count recurring threes. It's much better than counting sheep jumping over a fence. I always drop off to sleep the moment I've counted three hundred and thirty three

of them!'

With everybody squashed into
Professor Prime's study, they all ate a
large tea. There were scones with cream
and jam, cucumber sandwiches, and a
luscious chocolate cake. Then, when it
was all finished, Annie and the Professor
raced one another to see who could add
up large numbers the quickest. The
Professor was very good at this, of
course, as he had years of experience and
was very famous, but at the end of the
competition he rose to his feet and
bowed to Annie.

'You win,' he said. 'I may be Professor
Prime. I may be known from Bombay to
Bulawayo, from Texas to Tokyo. I may
have written ten books on the subject of
multiplication. But you, my dear Annie,
you win hands down. You are a greater

mathematical genius than I!'

Annie smiled modestly.

'I don't know how I do it,' she said quietly.

But *we* do—don't we?

*       *       *

As he bade farewell to Annie at the front door, the Professor promised that he would be in touch with her soon about something important.

'I shan't tell you just yet what it is,' he said. 'But you will hear about it soon. I promise you that.'

Annie was very curious as to what this might be, and for the next few days it was difficult for her to settle down to work. At the back of her mind was the Professor's promise. What could he possibly have in mind?

*       *       *

She did not have long to wait. At the end of that week a letter arrived from the Professor.

'Dear Annie,' he wrote. 'I have now

41

completed my plans for holding an international mathematical competition. The aim of this competition will be to find the person who has the quickest calculating mind in the world. There will only be three competitors. Yourself, of course; the famous Indian mathematician, Mrs Nandidrooka; and the American champion mathematician, Mr Willoughby Quick. I shall be the judge.

'I have persuaded some very generous people to donate a large prize for the winner, and to make sure that as many people as possible will be able to see the competition, it has been agreed that the whole event will be shown on television.'

Annie was delighted. The thought of being on television was most exciting, and now that she was so good at mathematics she was not in the slightest bit afraid of a competition. After all, it was all so easy. She never had to think very hard about any of the mathematical problems she was asked. It was as if the numbers were there all the time in her head. They just arranged themselves and came out as the right answer. It was all terribly simple.

# CHAPTER EIGHT

News of the great mathematical competition spread fast. Annie was soon featured in all the newspapers, and articles about her were published in all the magazines. Before long, people recognized her in the street and would point her out to their friends. Annie felt rather shy about this at first, but she soon got used to it.

The week before the competition, the other contestants arrived in town. There was a great deal of attention given to Mrs Nandidrooka, who appeared wearing a flowing red silk sari embroidered in gold thread with mathematical symbols.

Then there was Mr Willoughby Quick. He caused a great uproar of excitement when he arrived. A crowd of people stood four deep outside his hotel as the amazing American mathematician stepped from his taxi, muttering mathematical formulae under his breath. He paid no attention to

anything that was said to him—he was so busy with his private calculations. Every so often, even in the middle of a meal, he would take a piece of paper out of his pocket and do rapid calculations, just to check that some figure or other was right.

'He's very clever,' people said, nodding thoughtfully. 'Look at the size of his head! Just imagine the brains inside there.'

Annie saw the photographs of Mrs Nandidrooka and Mr Willoughby Quick. She wondered what they were like. Did they think of anything other than mathematics, or was that all that

44

they had in life? Did they dream of numbers (as Professor Prime did)? Did they think of mathematics in the bath?

Annie hoped that she would have the chance to meet the two other contestants. Yet when she went round to their hotels, they were either out or too busy to see her. Mr Willoughby Quick saw nobody (she was told) and Mrs Nandidrooka spent a lot of her time in bed, her head covered with cool towels. This meant that Annie still had no idea about what they were like.

'They're bound to beat me,' she said to her parents. 'They're sure to be much quicker.'

'Nonsense,' scoffed Annie's father. 'They'll be frightened of you. You're younger than they are and it's a well known fact that young people's minds are quicker than older people's.'

Annie was not convinced. The day of the great competition was drawing close and she had a terrible feeling within her that something dreadful was going to happen.

And it did. The very night before the competition, as Annie got ready for bed

she noticed that the calculator was not on the shelf where she normally kept it. She searched everywhere. She looked in her cupboard, under the bed, in every drawer, and then started the search all over again. But it was no use. The calculator had vanished.

Her heart heavy with dread, Annie went to bed without the calculator under her pillow. Perhaps it would turn up tomorrow, she thought; perhaps it will be all right if I sleep just one night without it under my pillow. Maybe its magic will last. But then again, maybe it wouldn't and if that happened, then the competition would be a complete and terrible disaster.

Immediately before she was due to go

to the television studio the next day, she asked her father to test her.

'But there's no need,' he said. 'We all know how good you are. You're never wrong these days—never.'

'I know,' said Annie. 'But please, just ask me a few questions.'

So Annie's father asked her a few questions, and Annie answered each of them as quickly and correctly as ever.

'There!' crowed her father. 'I told you that everything would be all right.'

He was quite confident that Annie would win the competition and be recognized as the quickest mathematician in the world. But Annie, for a reason which she could not tell anybody about, was not so sure.

\*　　　\*　　　\*

The television station was beset by reporters when Annie arrived. As she got out of her father's car and walked up the front steps, there was a great flashing of flash guns as the photographers all made sure of their picture for the front page of the next day's newspapers. Some of

Annie's friends were there too, and they cheered her as she went into the studio.

Annie turned and waved to her friends from the top of the steps, and just as she did so another car drew up at the bottom of the steps. The photographers all scurried into position as out of the car there stepped the glittering figure of Mrs Nandidrooka.

Annie watched as the famous Indian mathematician climbed up the steps towards her. As she approached, Annie stepped forward to greet her.

'Mrs Nandidrooka,' she began. 'It's a great honour to be competing against you, and I just wanted to say…'

Mrs Nandidrooka walked straight on. Not for a moment did she look at Annie, nor give any appearance of having heard her. In fact, she totally ignored her, rustling past in a shimmy of golden cloth.

Annie was dumbstruck. Mrs Nandidrooka had made her feel so small and unimportant. It was as if she thought it a great cheek for a girl of eleven to be challenging her. Well, maybe it was. Perhaps Professor Prime shouldn't have set up the competition in the first place.

As Annie was thinking this, another car arrived. This was a long car, that seemed to go on forever, and out of the very back, from what must have been the fifth row of seats, stepped the renowned Mr Willoughby Quick.

After what had happened with Mrs Nandidrooka, Annie was reluctant to go forward to greet Mr Willoughby Quick. But she need not have worried—he came up to her, shook her hand warmly, and patted her on the shoulder.

'Good try, kid!' he said. 'I like to see kids trying, even if they're bound to lose!'

And with that dispiriting remark, Mr

Willoughby Quick strode up the steps behind Annie and entered the studio. Annie, almost on the point of tears, dragged her feet up the remaining steps, hoping all the time that something would happen to stop the terrible ordeal that lay before her.

# CHAPTER NINE

Inside the television studio, Professor Prime was already sitting in his presenter's chair. Annie was shown to her seat, directly opposite the other two contestants, and was given instructions on how to look into the camera when she

spoke. Professor Prime gave her a little wave, which made her feel slightly better, but her heart was still performing all sorts of curious leaps within her.

'Quiet everybody!' the director shouted. 'One minute to go!'

'It's not too late to get up and walk out of the studio,' Annie told herself. 'Nobody could stop me.'

But then she thought of all her family and friends, watching the competition, and she realized what an awful disappointment it would be for them if the competition went on without her.

Now the programme had started. Professor Prime was introducing the contestants and, before Annie had the time to think about it much, the first question was being given to the contestants.

The question was very difficult indeed. It went:

'What is the result of 3,000,560 being multiplied by the number of days in 62 years (excluding Christmas)?'

At home, seated before their screens, all the people watching the competition gave a gasp. What a question! Surely nobody could answer that.

Annie closed her eyes. Yes. The answer was coming. She opened her eyes, looked in the direction of Professor Prime and gave the answer.

'Correct,' said Professor Prime. 'Absolutely right.'

The other two had not worked out the answer yet and they looked at Annie in a jealous sort of way.

'Beginner's luck,' muttered Mr Willoughby Quick under his breath.

'She won't be able to last at that rate,' said Mrs Nandidrooka to herself.

And as for Annie, she just thought: Thank goodness.

Professor Prime now turned to the next question. It was even more difficult than the first, involving all sorts of halves, thirds, quarters and even a few sixteenths. Once more, Annie closed her eyes and waited for the answer to come. Nothing happened. She closed her eyes again. This time, the answer came dimly and she stuttered it out.

She was correct. As Professor Prime congratulated her on her second correct answer, Annie mopped her brow with her handkerchief. She had hardly been able to see that number in her mind for some reason—and yet it had been right.

She glanced at Mrs Nandidrooka and Mr Willoughby Quick. Both the celebrated mathematicians were staring at her in a very unfriendly way.

'Now,' said Professor Prime. 'If Annie gets this one right, she will have won. So here we go.'

Annie listened to the question. It certainly sounded very hard. She closed her eyes and concentrated hard. Was a number coming into her mind? No. She frowned. Perhaps that would help. No. Nothing was coming. Nothing at all.

Back at home. Annie's family sat on the edge of their seats in front of the television.

'Come on, Annie!' cheered her father. 'You've answered harder ones than that before.'

And in their houses, all Annie's friends waited with bated breath.

'Annie,' they pleaded. 'Don't let us down now. Please don't.'

Annie clenched her fists under her table. Through the slit of her half-closed

54

eyes she could see Mrs Nandidrooka and Mr Willoughby Quick thinking hard—she would have to say something quickly if they were not to get in before her.

'3?' Annie suddenly blurted out. 'Is that the answer?'

Professor Prime looked at her in astonishment.

'I beg your pardon,' he said in a very surprised voice. 'Did you say 3?'

Annie nodded. 'Yes,' she said, but she knew it was wrong. In that terrible moment she knew that she was no longer a mathematical genius.

There was uproar in the studio when Annie gave her answer. Mrs

Nandidrooka threw up her hands and cackled with laughter. Mr Willoughby Quick took a handkerchief out of his pocket and waved it in the air exuberantly. Even Professor Prime, although puzzled at first, began to laugh.

Only Annie was silent. She had suspected that something like this was going to happen, and now it had.

# CHAPTER TEN

Mrs Nandidrooka won. It was a close thing between her and Mr Willoughby Quick, but eventually, on the final question, he came up with a wrong answer and she was declared the winner.

Annie answered no more questions. Indeed, now she had difficulty even in remembering what the questions were. Professor Prime looked at her expectantly from time to time, hoping that her old brilliance would reappear, but it did not.

'My dear girl,' he said at the end of the competition, 'what on earth happened to you?'

'I'm sorry,' said Annie, sounding quite miserable. 'I don't seem to be able to do mathematics any more.'

Professor Prime was very comforting.

'Don't worry,' he said. 'This sometimes happens to people. I knew a man who even forgot his two times table. It came back to him later, while he was swimming. It was a most curious affair.'

Annie slipped away while Mrs Nandidrooka and Mr Willoughby Quick were having an argument over one of the questions. All she wanted to do now was to forget about the whole business. She hoped that everybody who had been watching her would forget it too. She was not looking forward to facing all her school friends again on Monday.

How they would laugh at her!

\*     \*     \*

Annie's parents were very good about it

all.

'It doesn't matter in the slightest,' her father said. 'You did your best.'

'But it was so awful,' said Annie. 'All the figures disappeared from my mind— just like that!'

'Very strange,' said her mother. There was a silence. Then her father spoke again.

'Annie,' he said, 'have you any idea— any idea at all—how you became so good at mathematics in the first place?'

Annie looked down at the floor. She would have to tell them now.

'I've been sleeping with a calculator under my pillow,' she said. 'It seems to have made all the difference.'

Her father stared at her, his eyes wide with surprise.

'You mean with my little calculator?' he asked. 'With that funny little one you borrowed a few weeks ago?'

'Yes,' said Annie. 'It must be very special.'

'Oh dear,' said her father quietly, shaking his head. 'Oh dear! Oh dear!'

Annie wondered what her father meant, but she was soon to find out.

'I think I know why you aren't a mathematical genius any more,' he said. 'It's all my fault.'

'Why?' asked Annie. 'What have you done?'

'I've thrown the calculator away,' he said sadly. 'I bought two new calculators yesterday—one for you and one for me. And I found my old one in your room and decided that it was too old to keep. I threw it in the dustbin.'

'But we could get it out,' Annie said. 'It might still be there.'

Annie's father jumped to his feet. 'We could try,' he shouted out. 'The men might not have emptied the bins yet. Hurry!'

They ran downstairs and out of the house as fast as they could. The rubbish bins, which everybody had to put out at their gates for emptying, were still standing there. Annie picked up a lid and looked inside. It was empty. And there, at the end of the road, was the rubbish truck turning the corner and driving away.

'Well,' she said to her father. 'At least we tried.'

Annie had thought that that was the end of her ability to do mathematics, but it was not quite. Certainly she was not a mathematical genius any more, but fortunately, a little bit of the calculator's magic had remained in her head and soon came back to her. She could no longer do the amazing, difficult sums that she had been able to do before, but she was delighted to find out that she could now do more or less what all the other children could do. No longer did she give the wrong money in shops; no longer did she get everything so hopelessly wrong. Annie, in fact, had become just about average at mathematics, which suited her very well.

It was very strange at first, not having the numbers come mysteriously into her mind. But after a while, she discovered that it was much more fun to be able to do mathematics properly, and this made her feel quite proud of herself. Now that she could actually add, she found that she enjoyed it. Mathematics, it seemed to Annie, was really not so bad after all!

She was also most relieved when she went back to school and discovered that nobody really minded about what had happened in the competition.

'You did very well to begin with,' the people at school all said. 'We were really proud of you. But you had no chance against that horrible woman and that dreadful man.'

The head teacher also congratulated her.

'You were a credit to us,' she said. 'It doesn't matter in the least that your mind went blank later on.'

'But I'm no longer so good at mathematics,' she said. 'And I'll never be that good again.'

The head teacher laughed. 'There's no reason why that should worry you,' she said.

'But what about exams?' said Annie. 'I may not find them as hard as I found them before, but they'll still be quite difficult.'

'You've passed your mathematics examination, remember,' said the head teacher, smiling. 'There are no more exams left for you to take—at least in mathematics.'

'I see,' said Annie, beginning to understand. It was a marvellous thought. She would never have to do mathematics exams again, and she still knew enough about numbers to get by perfectly well. It was all very pleasant.

Annie could have leapt in the air with delight. In fact, once the head teacher had turned to walk away, that's exactly what she did.

And as she jumped, she thought of a

mathematical puzzle. If a girl jumps into the air four times a minute for twelve minutes, then how many jumps does she jump altogether?

'Yes, that's it,' said Annie to herself. '48.'

Was she right? Now, let's think...